Run, Rasputin Run!

by

Jennifer Miller

Illustrated by

Vanessa Knight

Note for Librarians: A cataloguing record for this book is available from Library and Archives
Canada at www.collectionscanada.ca/amicus/index-e.html
ISBN 1-4120-6430-9

*Printed in Victoria, BC, Canada. Printed on paper with minimum 30% recycled fibre. Trafford's print shop
runs on "green energy" from solar, wind and other environmentally-friendly power sources.*

Offices in Canada, USA, Ireland and UK

This book was published *on-demand* in cooperation with Trafford Publishing. On-demand
publishing is a unique process and service of making a book available for retail sale to the
public taking advantage of on-demand manufacturing and Internet marketing. On-demand
publishing includes promotions, retail sales, manufacturing, order fulfilment, accounting and
collecting royalties on behalf of the author.

Book sales for North America and international:
Trafford Publishing, 6E–2333 Government St.,
Victoria, BC v8t 4p4 CANADA
phone 250 383 6864 (toll-free 1 888 232 4444)
fax 250 383 6804; email to orders@trafford.com
Book sales in Europe:
Trafford Publishing (uk) Ltd., Enterprise House, Wistaston Road Business Centre,
Wistaston Road, Crewe, Cheshire cw2 7rp UNITED KINGDOM
phone 01270 251 396 (local rate 0845 230 9601)
facsimile 01270 254 983; orders.uk@trafford.com
Order online at:
trafford.com/05-1341

10 9 8 7 6 5 4 3

CAST of CHARACTERS

Mr. Owl – wise and the overseer to all the little creatures of the forest, finds himself in a struggle to save a little bear cub and a mouse, about to be eaten up by Old Rasputin, the wolf.

Heathcliff – happy to be alive and a playful hare, always out in the night, chasing his friends in many hours of fun and games.

Mr. Mouse – the spunky mouse, who seems to always end up in some sort of danger. Can he be rescued this time? Or, has his luck run out?

Daisy – Mr. Owl's mate ... comes upon a very strange sight one night involving Mr. Owl and little Heathcliff. Is there any way she can help save them and try to keep Mr. Mouse and the little cub, Sasha, from being eaten up by mean, Old Rasputin?

Mr. Possum – Short-legged and not very brave, he befriends the little cub. Will he find the courage to stay and help the mouse and cub escape, or will he turn his back in fear and run to safety?

Sasha – the little cub, left to wander the night alone, after his ancestors are shot by poachers. Can he survive, alone and lost, or will Old Rasputin have his way and eat him up?

Rasputin – the mean, old wolf, who is feared by every living creature in the forest. Cocky and arrogant, he torments them all with his piercing howls, chuckling at the fear he spreads throughout the land. He is the king of the forest! Yes siree! This night, he will not be outsmarted! He'll have the cub and the mouse! He is hungry and will have his dinner!

This story takes place in the forests of Netherland.

I dedicate my book "Run, Rasputin Run!" to my Mom and Dad with love, appreciation, and precious memories that will last us all a lifetime.

Contents

A CRY in the FOREST

The wise, old owl squinted through the darkness. He knew he had heard something different from the usual sounds of the night. He cocked his head from one side to the other, intense and as still as the branch on which he sat. *Ha!* he thought. *There it is again.*

He lowered his large head, his eyes wide as they scanned the tree-lined forest underneath him. Soft, muffled sobs reached his ears through the brush below. He flew down, closer to where the cries came from.

His gaze held on a wee bear cub who sat in a heap against a worn tree trunk, his fur matted with honey and twigs, his face sad and frightened. Puzzled that this little cub was all alone, with no sign of its family close by, the owl guessed that they were probably killed by poachers he saw hunting in the forests lately. He knew this little one had outsmarted them somehow by hiding out of sight until they left.

He lifted his foot, scratching his head in bewilderment as he wondered how to help. The cry of a lone wolf broke the stillness of the night, sending fear to all the creatures out roaming about who were looking for food. The owl frowned with worry...he recognized *that* howl.

"That's that mean Old Rasputin, out looking for any trouble he can find."

1

Every living creature shook with fear as they made their way quickly back to the safety of their dens before the evil, old wolf could catch them and eat them up.

The fierce howl came again, this time drawing closer. He eyed the little cub, which was lost and defenseless. A noise in the brush below brought back the attention of the wise, old owl. Glancing away quickly from the little bear, he saw Old Rasputin slowly creep through the brush. His belly was close to the ground as he drew

nearer to where the little bear sat. Smacking his mouth hungrily, he was already tasting his evening meal.

The owl tensed. He flapped his large wings back and forth angrily, hoping to scare the wolf away, his huge eyes flaring at the arrogant

beast. Rasputin stretched out comfortably. He knew the owl was trying his best to frighten him off, and he grinned wickedly in response. Well, he would show that silly bird a thing or two.

"No-one frightens this wolf," he chuckled. He had his meal directly within reach and no-one was going

3

to take it away. "Nosiree," he said to himself as he watched the owl in the tree above him. He slowly raised his heavy, lidded eyes to mock the troublesome old pest.

The owl stared back in hostility, his large beak making clicking sounds. He was ready to attack. Rasputin looked away, not quite so sure of himself now.

"Ummph! So, this is the game you wish to play," he growled. "I have all the time in the world, but *you* have only until daybreak when you can no longer see. When your eyesight leaves you, I'll have my dinner...or breakfast," he grinned. "But, no matter. I'll have my belly full while you'll have nothing."

He stretched out lazily with his head resting on his paws, watching the little bear with contented glee, unafraid of the taunting owl.

The wise owl knew what Rasputin was thinking. The fact that it was true made him jumpy. He'd have to do something before daylight set in to save this little bear - morning was approaching and he hadn't much time.

The owl started to put his plan to work while not taking his eyes off the old wolf.

A NIGHTLY RACE

Mr. Mouse ran through the brush with Heathcliff, the hare, on their nightly race. Each would challenge the other with their racing skills, hoping to win. In and out of the bushes they ran, hopping up and down and laughing into the night. Both squealed with happiness as they went crashing to the ground.

"Ah! I won!" laughed Mr. Mouse, jumping up onto the hare's back, tugging at the long ears of his friend. "Now it's your turn to treat me to a night out on the town!"

Heathcliff jumped up, pulling the tail of his little friend. "Right you are! 'Twas a fine race indeed," he laughed. "A night out on the town it is!"

"I tell you what," squealed the mouse. "You wait right here while I go fetch me some cheese from my cupboard at home. Winning a race makes me hungry," he yelled, racing off. He stopped after a few yards, looking gleefully back at his friend. "I forgot! I'll bring back a carrot or two," he teased,

racing back off into the night.

Heathcliff grinned after his silly friend. "Don't be too long!" he yelled. "I thought I heard that mean Old Rasputin while we were playing."

"I won't," answered Mr. Mouse, his voice trailing off in the distance. "I'll be back before you can say 'Hippety Hop!'"

Heathcliff sat down again, stretching himself out with his paws behind his head, staring into the night sky. He was happy he had such a good friend, silly as he was and all. He smiled, already tasting the carrots Mr. Mouse promised to bring back with him.

Mr. Mouse, delighted at finally winning a race with his friend, darted in and out of the heavy brush, anxious to pack up some cheese and carrots and then hurry back to his friend, who was waiting for his return. After they ate then they would run again, enjoying their night out on the town.

Faster and faster he ran, with not a worry in the world, when he ran smack into the sad little cub, scaring him so much that both went tumbling to the ground. The mouse hung on for dear life as they rolled over and over down the hill towards the edge of a cliff. They flew through the air, finally hitting the ground with a thud, then tumbling further into an old abandoned well. They bounced off the sides into total blackness.

Hanging on tighter, Mr. Mouse dug deeper into the little cub's fur as on and on they continued to tumble, finally hitting bottom and coming to an abrupt halt right into a sleeping possum.

Mr. Mouse scurried out of harm's way, shaken and filthy and muttering angrily to himself. Mr. Possum jumped to his feet, wide awake now and very mad at these intruders. He glared at the large ball of fur that dared to awaken him from a peaceful sleep, scowling down at the tattered cub while brushing off his fur.

"Have you no mercy? Waking someone up like that could kill them!" he stormed.

The little cub still lay in a heap, thinking what a terrible time he was having. Cautiously, he eyed the angry possum, deciding that maybe he

wouldn't answer until this creature calmed down. *And besides,* he thought, *I am too weary to get up, let alone argue with this short-legged whatever-it-is.*

"Hmmph!" the possum huffed, moving carefully away from the cub, seeking another place in which to go back to sleep. Mr. Mouse watched the possum amble away. Seeing it was safe to venture out, he marched over to the little cub, jumping upon a rock to make better eye contact.

"Hey!" he shrieked, "Now look and see what you've done!" He stared into the cub's eyes with his paws firmly planted on his hips, foot tapping impatiently.

Too exhausted to say anything, the little cub eyed the critter who was really to blame for all of this. Sighing sadly, he closed his eyes. Perhaps, if he ignored the mouse, he would stop his ramblings and let them both get some rest from the ordeal they just went through.

Knowing it was useless to argue with this oaf, Mr. Mouse jumped off the rock and huddled into some twigs, tired as well but eyeing the little bear with distaste.

8

"All your fault," he muttered with gritted teeth. "If you had been home in bed where you belonged - not out wandering all alone in the night - nary a care in the world, this wouldn't have happened - no thought for the safety of others. If it weren't for you, I'd be back with my friend, enjoying our night out on the town - oh Heathcliff!" he jumped up, wondering how to get out of this well. He scurried back and forth around the bottom of the hole he was in until he slowly sank wearily to the ground once more.

Hopeless! he thought. Maybe Heathcliff would come looking for him when he didn't return with the cheese and carrots. Again he scowled at the now sleeping cub. "All your fault," he repeated. Hearing the screech of an owl nearby he shuddered, creeping gently over next to the bear to snuggle into the warmth of his fur. Feeling safe for the moment, he curled into a tiny ball and slept.

CRIES from the WELL

The wise, old owl saw the bear go tumbling down the hill, the mouse hanging on as both went sailing through the air, crashed to the ground, and rolled into the abandoned well. *Now you've gotten yourselves into a fine mess*, the owl thought.

Hearing cries coming from the well he flew closer, landing on a tree branch that overhung the pit they had fallen into. Peering down into the hole he saw the bear all curled up, soft moans coming from his restless sleep. He stretched his large  head further, catching sight of the mouse lying next to him, snuggled deep into the fur of the bear. To comfort them he began making soft cooing sounds, especially to the little bear - as he was not only abandoned, all alone and scared, but had such a time of it this night he needed all the comforting he could get.

The owl looked tentatively around, making sure none of his friends were watching him. He'd be the laughing stock of the forest if word got out – especially to his friend and mate Daisy, who would laugh and tell all their other friends in the forest of this. *Certainly not good for my tough image*, he grimaced. Soon, Daisy would be joining him here. He'd keep a watchful eye out for her. He wouldn't be at their usual tree where they always met but, when he saw her approaching, he'd call out. She'd know his call.

His gaze turned back to the well, seeing his cooing sounds had the effect he hoped for. The little bear stopped his twitching and moans and both the mouse and little cub slept peacefully ... at least for the moment.

HEATHCLIFF'S SEARCH

Heathcliff sighed, wondering what was taking Mr. Mouse so long coming back. Fog started to roll in, making it difficult to see through the brush. Strange sounds of the night brought worried glances as all the animals nervously peeked out from their little beds.

Heathcliff grew restless. Mr. Mouse was out there somewhere and he started to worry that his friend was in dire trouble. It just wasn't like him to be so late, since every night they played together until the dawn set in. He peered through the brush - there was no sign of his friend. Overhead,

he saw several owls fly off into the night. *I hope Mr. Mouse is all right*, he thought.

He twitched his nose nervously. Hopping out of the thicket, he looked around the best he could.

"Mr. Mouse?" he whispered. "Where are you?"

Quietly he waited, hoping for a sound from his silly little friend ... but there was nothing. Heathcliff's fur was getting very wet from the fog and

he was starting to grow cold.

"Mr. Mouse! Where are you?" he called out once more. Shivering now from the cold, he shook his fur to dry it a little from the dampness. *I'll just have to search for Mr. Mouse myself then.*

Starting in the direction where Mr. Mouse had raced away, he kept a watchful eye and ear. He would find his friend before the night was over and would no doubt have some story to tell of his happenings. Meanwhile, he hoped his friend was not in trouble or badly hurt.

Missing his friend made him very worried. Besides, if his friend was out walking the forest that night with him he'd have someone to talk to and not be so afraid of the eerie sounds he was hearing.

As he walked deeper into the woods, he kept calling out softly to Mr. Mouse. The night got colder, so he pulled his ears down tighter against his neck to keep out the wind, walking onward.

••

Mr. Owl knew he had to do something - and fast. Soon, the sun would come up as morning approached. He hadn't much time to save the baby cub, and now, the mouse. Old Rasputin was right: come daylight he wouldn't be able to see, and the little animals in the well would be all eaten up. Wolves could get in and out of places most other creatures couldn't. Mean, Old Rasputin would have his breakfast and be on his way.

The old owl let out a screech that shook the night forest like a cannon and Heathcliff leaped into a pile of leaves, his nose twitching as fast as his heart was racing. The owl spotted Heathcliff and flew closer to where he was huddled in the deep brush.

"Heathcliff?" he asked, "What are you doing out here at this hour, cold and shivering on this foggy night? Why aren't you in your lair, safe and warm?"

"D-don't go s-scaring me like that!" Heathcliff shakily replied as he brushed himself off. "To answer your question, I'm looking for my friend, Mr. Mouse."

"Aha!" answered the old owl. "Well, I just happen to know where he is!"

"You do?" Heathcliff shook with excitement. "Is he alright? Is he hurt? Where is he and why didn't he return? I waited and waited while he was getting some cheese and carrots and when he never returned ... I just knew he was in some bad trouble."

"Hold on there," the owl softly muttered. "One question at a time. First of all, your friend Mr. Mouse is safe for the time being, but fell into an abandoned well while hanging onto a bear cub. He doesn't appear to want to leave the little cub alone." He squinted at Heathcliff. "And *you* look awful."

Heathcliff sat up with as much dignity as he could manage and started brushing his coat and fur clean. "I have had a nasty night of it, I'll have you know; and, fearing for my friend, taking tumbles when someone screeches like a half-crazed ghost into the night. I lost my balance seeking cover to hide and that makes for a decrepit appearance," he replied, embarrassed and a tad impatient with this pristine owl.

"Now, now," soothed the old owl. "You'll clean up just fine. Meanwhile, there is a task we must face. Old Rasputin is determined to have both your little mouse friend and the little cub for dinner! If we don't act fast, I might add, he will!" he scowled.

"Come on then, let's go!" Heathcliff shouted, tugging at the owl's wing. "We must hurry and save them before it's too late!"

HEATHCLIFF'S INJURY

Old Rasputin had heard the frightening cry of the owl. Quickly, he glanced up into the trees around him and was surprised to not see the old bird. Only one thing bothered him: he suspected that the owl had gone to bring back all his feathered reinforcements. He could fight one, but a dozen owls nipping at his flanks kind of bothered him.

A storm was coming - Rasputin knew that with all this wind and heavy fog coming in. The sound of loud thunder roared off in the distance and, feeling some rain starting to fall, he got to his feet, shaking out his fur.

Winter was here and he didn't much like these heavy storms rolling through - never knew when a tree might topple on him. And with all this fog, it was hard to tell what was brewing out there.

He peered down into the well. It was mighty deep with not much to hang on to. Looking around, he spotted a fallen tree. *Now*, he mused, *if I can just drag it over and knock it into the well, I'll be a lot happier.*

Pawing at the dead stump, he began to form an idea. It was not too big to handle and, if he could do it, he would have his meal waiting below and be on his way before that nasty owl returned.

Biting into one of the smaller branches, he backed up, pulling the tree slowly toward the well. Old Rasputin grunted and growled, gnawing at the branch while digging his front feet deeper into the ground. He tugged harder, spitting out broken pieces of the branch. His face became sweaty and dirty, and he scowled at the bits of bark sticking between his teeth.

Off in the distance he heard the owls.

"More than a couple," he muttered. Soon he would have a bunch of screaming birds trying to take away his dinner.

On and on, Old Rasputin worked at pulling the dead tree closer to the well. Inch by inch, he gained momentum and gradually pulled it close enough to get it down into the hole. Not daring to stop and rest he continued his hard work. He'd have to be careful not to get so close he might accidentally fall in.

"Ahh!" he grinned. "Almost finished and dinner almost on the table."

His head rose to the sky and he let out a joyous cry into the air with wild abandon, his stomach happy with the thought of a hearty meal on the way.

■■■

Meanwhile, Heathcliff and Mr. Owl hurried through the forest, the owl flying overhead and keeping a close watch on the rabbit below. Hippety-hop went Heathcliff, stretching his legs as far as they could go and gaining speed with every bound. Thankful the owl was leading the way, Heathcliff raced on, following on land and always close behind.

"Watch that tree!" screeched the owl, whipping his head back in time to see Heathcliff run smack into it.

19

The owl shook his head with frustration and circled high overhead, making sure this clumsy hare was all right. What he saw when he gazed down was a stunned Heathcliff, lying in a heap.

Stretching his wings, he glided slowly to the ground, landing next to the dazzed hare. Flapping his wings against the rabbit's back, he jumped up and down, trying to wake his little friend.

"Heathcliff!" he shouted, "Wake up!"

Not hearing a reply he cradled the hare's body with his wing and lowered his head closer to look right into Heathcliff's weary face - still no movement, no sounds either.

Hearing a noise in the brush next to them, he spread his free wing out to shield the rabbit from the cold and whatever predator lingered close by.

Afraid that Heathcliff was injured, he raised his head and let out three piercing screams ... the code of the forest - the cry for help!

Heathcliff shook, terrified with all this racket. He slowly came awake from his nasty spill and tried to get up, only to find a pair of warm wings were holding him down. His heart pounded fiercely as his mind panicked. *Someone has hold of me and is going to kill me! Then Mr. Mouse will never be rescued!*

He let out a squeal, trying with all his strength to escape the grip on him.

"Hold still!" the owl scolded. "It's me! It's good to see you awake! Now, lie here for a few minutes, calm down some, then we'll be on our way again. Are you hurt? Is anything broken?"

He stared at Heathcliff, impatient, but concerned.

"I can't breathe," Heathcliff spat, indignantly. Your big wing in my face is smothering me."

21

The owl chuckled, glad he had his friend back again. Loosening his grip, he pulled back his wing while eyeing Heathcliff carefully. "Can you get up?"

Heathcliff tried, but fell to one side. Once more he tried, this time standing and holding his left foot off the ground. He took a step, then fell again, landing next to Mr. Owl.

"It seems you injured your foot," the owl soothed, but he was not too happy with these latest events and, knowing all too well they had to rescue the cub and Mr. Mouse, the owl looked at his little friend and his injured leg worriedly.

"Is it your leg or is it your foot?" he asked.

"It's my foot!" Heathcliff stormed. "But we still must find Mr. Mouse. We must save him before it's too late!" He tugged on the owl's wing but had to sit down again, looking worn and tattered.

"Let's have a look then." Mr. Owl bent his head, peering closely at the rabbit's foot. He pecked around the area with his large beak, trying to find the exact spot that hurt.

"OUCH!!" squealed the hare. "That hurts!"

"Okay. Relax and let me check you. Ah here ... a sharp twig has cut into your foot."

He bit into the small fragment and pulled hard, jerking back with the twig in his beak. Heathcliff let out a painful yell, almost kicking the owl over.

"Are you crazy?!"

"There, there," the owl soothed, "it's out. You'll be okay. Now, jump on my back and off we'll go!"

Heathcliff groaned. "I can't fly."

"Oh, yes you can," the owl replied.

"No, I can't!" the hare yelled back, "Even watching squirrels climb and jump from tree to tree makes me afraid."

"Get on my back," Mr. Owl insisted, ignoring the furry one's fear. He watched and, seeing the stubborn hare's attitude, nudged him none too gently.

"Now!"

MR. OWL – The PILOT

Hearing all the approaching owls in the distance, Heathcliff jumped on, his paws wrapped firmly around the owl's neck.

"Not too tight," chided the owl. "I have to breathe."

Hearing his approaching friends and hoping Daisy was not one of them - for fear of being humiliated - he grumbled, "I have had better nights!"

"What?" Heathcliff asked, fright in his voice. He hated this idea and really didn't want to do flying stuff at all. The only thing that kept him from

leaping off and hopping back into the thicket was the thought of his friend being in serious trouble.

Sensing Heathcliff's fear of flying, the owl turned his head around, looking directly into this hare's fearful face whose eyes were wide with terror. His little feet dug deeper into his wings.

"I *will* get you there, safe and sound. We *will* save your little friend. My friends *will* soon be here to help fend off Old Rasputin; but first, you must let go of my wings. Once I'm in the air flying, wrap your feet around my chest and hang on tight. You won't fall. Trust me!"

25

Heathcliff did as he was instructed and off they flew, the rabbit hanging on for dear life, closing his eyes so he wouldn't see he was off the ground.

Mr. Owl scowled. What a sight they must be. Heathcliff was a brave little guy to fly with him. He had to give him some praise for that. This was not a good night all around - certainly not what he and Daisy had planned. "Sure hope she doesn't see this" he murmured.

But Mr. Owl's main concern right now was saving the cub and Mr. Mouse. He knew Heathcliff's foot would mend, as it was only a small cut; and now, with the sliver from the twig removed, it would heal fast. Meanwhile, the weight on his back was slowing him down. He spread his wings further, trying to gain speed.

Heathcliff, feeling the fanning out and the speed picking up, held on tighter and squeezed his eyes tighter still. His heart raced so fast he thought he would die.

"Calm yourself down back there!" the owl reprimanded. "When this night is over and you're out playing with Mr. Mouse again, this will all seem like a dream."

"I w-wish it were," shrieked the hare, wrapping his feet closer into the owl's breast.

Mr. Owl chuckled, happy the hare was feeling a little better. Soon his friends would be close behind and all would be well; he sure hoped it would be that way anyway, as he was getting more worried himself - daylight was fast approaching. Time was running out. Could he rescue the cub and Mr. Mouse before they were eaten up by mean, Old Rasputin?

He didn't know.

He just flew toward the abandoned well and hoped he'd arrive in time.

RASPUTIN ENTERS the WELL

Old Rasputin pulled harder, satisfied that soon he would get down into the abandoned well and have his belly full - which by now was very, very empty. He smacked his lips with glee.

Stopping to rest, he happily looked down into the hole. "Sleep well, little feast," he grinned. "Soon, I will have you for my dinner."

He did one last final tug on the log, setting it in place down into the well with a solid kick of his back leg. The log end slammed to the bottom of the hole with a heavy thud. Satisfied that he could now climb down into the well and also climb out before those silly owls returned, Rasputin happily started his descent into the deep hole.

One step ... two steps, he counted out in his mind, backing down into the well, his paws tightly wrapped around the battered log. He wasn't sure he liked the idea of backing down here tail-first, but it was his only chance of getting to the bottom safely at this angle.

His hind legs felt each step carefully, not wanting to wake the cub.

The heavy fog was bad enough, making it hard to see where he was going, but the log was slippery from all the dampness. He had to be very cautious and, not wanting to work too hard for his meal before him, try to be

28

as quiet as possible.

He looked up where he had started to climb.

"Almost halfway there," he grinned.

Pieces of the dead tree fell off as each step he took loosened the bark. He scowled through his clenched teeth, hoping it wouldn't wake his dinner up.

He waited before taking another step, listening for any movement below him. There was none. It seemed the bear slept on, just wanting this night to be over and then be on his way back to his lair.

In the distance he heard the approaching owls.

"Drat!" he muttered sharply. "If they think they are going to take away my dinner, they have another thought coming. They can't outsmart Old Rasputin - No Sirree!"

• •

Mr. Mouse awoke with a start as a piece of bark noisily landed next to where he and the little cub slept. His nose twitching nervously, then he jumped up on the cub's back, startled and alert.

"Someone is up there!" he gasped. Seeing the tree log lowered down into the well made him very nervous. Tapping his foot, he sure wished Heathcliff was here with him. Together they would figure out what to do. He was scared and not afraid to admit it. He smelled the smell of danger and knew that trouble was on it's way down that log. Someone was planning to eat the cub and himself for their evening meal. Well, he

29

would just have to wake the cub and maybe they could both find a way to save themselves from whoever was climbing down that log to eat them up.

He glanced at the little cub, who stared at him with curiosity.

"You're awake!" Mr. Mouse whispered in a quick rush.

"Aaah!" the cub answered back in surprise.

"Can't you talk?" the little mouse asked, frustrated and in need of some conversation.

"Yes?" nervously replied the cub.

"Great!" the mouse jumped up and down, waving his arms about him with excitement. "Did you hear all the noise?"

The little cub nodded, solemn and dejected as he looked up into where daylight would be coming soon. "Yes. I heard someone trying to come down here and eat us both. We are his meal and here we are – trapped - no place to run for cover, and no place to hide. We are doomed." The little bear shrugged his shoulders sadly as he looked at Mr. Mouse. Then, he turned and sank his head wearily down on his paws, lost and forlorn.

"Are you crazy?" the mouse shrieked, agitated and greatly impatient. "Do you intend to just lie here and be eaten up?"

The little cub yawned dejectedly, telling the mouse his sorrowful story. "There's nothing we can do. These last few days have not been happy ones. I have seen my mother and father killed, I've been roaming around these woods until I am lost, I can't find my way back home - that is no longer home anyway, but a place where at least I don't get lost and the trees and noises of the night are friendly and recognizable, and I don't have a family to go back to or friends to play with. They are all dead or gone." The cub tearfully sighed, "There is nothing else that could be worse. I am tired and before I am eaten up, I just want to rest."

Cupping his paws over his eyes, the little cub slept.

Mr. Mouse jumped off the back of the sleeping cub, running over to come face to face with his new-found friend.

"Hey! Wake up!" he shrieked.

He stared into the bear's large nostrils. Running around in circles, he wondered how to get his attention.

"Ahhh!" he said as he jumped up and climbed onto the cub's nose. "Hey! Wake up!" He pinched the big nose. "You can't give up now! Wake up!"

He kept pinching the cub's nose as he yelled. The little cub wriggled his nose harshly, trying to throw off the little pest. He tossed his head from side to side but the mouse hung on.

"I won't let you give up!"

"Let go of my nose, you squeaky, little pest. Save yourself, but all is lost for me. I have no-one."

Mr. Mouse bit onto the bear's nose.

"YOWW!!" wailed the cub "Let go!

32

Are you crazy?" He pawed his nose.

"No!" replied the tiny creature. "It's time you come to your senses!"

"What for?" the cub asked.

Mr. Mouse thought for a second, then said, "I have a lot of friends. I'll introduce you to all of them and you'll like them," he tugged a bit harder. "but right now we must save ourselves."

"I am a bear cub. Playing with a bunch of mice doesn't appeal to me," grumbled the cub, rolling over on his side.

"Oh, but I have all kinds of playmates," happily shrieked the mouse. "Owls, hares, wild pigs, squirrels, deer and all the others. The only ones we have to look out for are the wolves … especially Old Rasputin. He's the meanest one in the forest, and always looking for a meal whether he's hungry or not. Everyone fears him. He's mean and likes being feared."

Mr. Mouse stood tall, chest stuck out bravely. "Why, I even know some bears who would accept you into their family. I *know* they would."

"And w-why would they do that?" stammered the cub.

"Because!!! That's why!!!" stormed the mouse. "But first you must wake up."

He pulled on the cub's ear, looking up. Something was still slowly climbing down and, if his hunch was right, it was that mean, old Rasputin. His little teeth started to chatter with fear. "Heathcliff, I need you!"

He jumped up to the bear's ear, biting into it with all the

33

strength he could muster. The little cub let out a bellow, jumping straight to his feet.

"Have you lost your senses!" he yelled, staring at the fallen mouse before him. Mr. Mouse jumped back onto his feet, lazily dusted himself off, then indignantly eyed the cub.

"Well, at least I have your attention!"

He pointed up to Old Rasputin slowly making his descent as the fog and slippery log were his enemies now. The little cub snorted. This didn't look good. No, it didn't. He stared at the little pest that seemed happy only when he was chewing on his nose or ear.

"You see?!" Mr. Mouse exclaimed. "We have to think of a way to save ourselves, and fast! That's Old Rasputin's behind, climbing down to claim his feast – US!"

LITTLE CUB and MR. MOUSE

The little cub wriggled from side to side, wishing he had a tree to scratch his back on. When he got nervous his back itched. He eyed the little mouse, staring open-mouthed back at him, agitated and probably not understanding his back needing scratching.

He looked up at the approaching wolf, then back at the mouse. "We have no way out and we are doomed," he said.

Mr. Mouse jumped onto the cub's back, heading for his ear again.

"NO! No more biting," he grunted. "If you scratch my back some, I will try to think of a way to outsmart that mean, old wolf."

He turned some to try and see the mouse, still swaying from side to side. Mr. Mouse couldn't believe this oaf of a bear. Their lives were in dire

trouble - soon to be eaten up, and this slowpoke wanted his back scratched.

The little bear saw his impatience.

"When I am nervous, even scared, my back itches. I have to find a tree to scratch it on, then I can think clearer." He stared into the frustrated mouse's eyes. "Not before."

Mr. Mouse started the scratching, slowly at first - then, to hurry things up, he went faster and faster, his little feet working together in a quick rhythm to ease the cub's itch.

35

Contented sighs filled the dark hole. Happy, throated sounds echoed throughout as the little bear was in ecstasy, still moving from side to side, lost in oblivion as tree bark from Rasputin's descent fell around them.

"That's enough, now. Thank you, Mr. Mouse," he happily said. "You made me very happy indeed. My mother scratched me like that when I was very little - too little to leave her side and find a tree."

His face lit up with joy, he thought for a minute as he studied his still-frantic friend. "We have very little time. What can we do?" he calmly asked.

"Don't you ever get excited?" stormed the trembling mouse. "This is not a picnic outing with a jar of honey! We are about to be eaten up and all you want is a back- rub!" Tapping his little foot, he looked up. Rasputin was more than halfway down. Soon, he would be upon them and have his meal.

"You could have run and saved yourself but you didn't. Why?" asked the little cub, content now and wanting to help his new friend.

Exasperated, the mouse softly replied, "We fell into this hole together, we must stay and try to get out. Together. 'Tis the way of the forest."

"Oh," smiled the cub. "Then let's try to think of something we can do to trick Old Rasputin. I have my size - not too big, but bigger than you," he grinned. "You have the courage and fight in you." He watched the little mouse, adding with glee, "You can always bite his ear!"

Mr. Mouse paced back and forth in front of the cub. Hearing the last comment, he scowled up into the cub's face. Then his face lit up.

"Hey! That's it!" He jumped up and down, pulling on the cub's fur and smiling from ear to ear. The bear smiled too, happy he had a new friend: small as he was, still a friend and such a good one.

He nudged into the mouse's head, forgetting his strength ... and the little mouse went tumbling down again. Both were so caught up in their new excitement and happiness in having a friend and their hopes of getting out, that they continued to play, teasing and enjoying this moment free from worry and sadness.

Old Rasputin didn't forget though.

He made the last step down onto the bottom of the well, grinning from thinking of his soon-to-be meals.

"Let them play," he chuckled to himself, quietly stretching his legs from all the climbing and the cold. He tensed his whole body, smacking his lips, and with the speed of lightning made his last and final jump on top of the little cub. Now it was his screams of joy and victory filling the night, howling out from the old abandoned well to the forest high above.

DAISY'S PLIGHT

The wise, old owl heard Rasputin's piercing screams that echoed throughout the forest. He knew right away that he was too late in rescuing the cub and Mr. Mouse. Maybe, if he flew faster, he could reach them before they were eaten up.

Turning his head around to look into the frightened face of Heathcliff, he shouted into the wind, trying to be heard through the thunder high overhead. "Hang on, Heathcliff! We don't have much time!"

Heathcliff yelled back, "That was Mr. Mouse! I know his scream! Those other screams must be the bear cub. Hurry!" Heathcliff dug in deeper, eyes shut, nose twitching. He always shuddered when he became scared - he was scared now, but he had to help save his friend and be strong.

"Hurry!" he cried again.

The owl stretched wide his wings, gaining speed as the wind roared on.

••

Daisy wondered why Mr. Owl hadn't shown up. He must be in some kind of trouble. With all this wind and heavy fog, it was hard to see what was happening in the forest. Lifting her head, she listened.

Nothing. Well, she would just have to fly around and look for her friend. Spanning her wings wide, she lifted off the branch of her meeting tree and gracefully flew around in a wide arc, looking ahead and far below. She flew far and wide, hoping to spot Mr. Owl. This was not a good night to be out.

She could barely see the trees. If she wasn't careful she could even fly right into one. Why, not too long ago, her friend broke her neck, flying around on a night like this. She didn't see the large oak and flew right into it.

"Poor Belle!" she thought aloud. "I miss our good times together, teasing and chasing the hawks." Now she had her friend, Mr. Owl, but she still missed Belle.

Flying around, she scanned the forest carefully, her eyes opened wide as dinner plates, flying in and out of the tree-lined area. Heavy moisture weighted her wings. She made a high dive, shaking off her feathers. It was hard to dry them but she did the best she could.

Circling and arcing into the wind she flew, diving toward the ground, caught up in the games of flight. She scolded herself. "I must find Mr. Owl."

Strengthening her wings, she continued her search, flying straight into the path of Mr. Owl. She swerved fiercely to one side, overjoyed to

40

find her friend. She also spotted Heathcliff riding on his back, looking scared and hanging on hard.

She gaped, beak open wide in shock.

"Mr. Owl! Just what do you think you are doing?" she stormed. Did you forget we were supposed to meet at the tree this night? I have never seen anything so ridiculous in my life! So, you're taxiing rabbits around now?"

"No time to explain now, Daisy. Mr. Mouse is in serious trouble, along with a bear cub. You remember Mr. Mouse?"

Hearing all the commotion, Heathcliff opened his eyes and looked right at Daisy.

"Daisy!" he cried.

"Heathcliff, is that you? What on earth are you doing riding atop Mr. Owl? Surely, you'll hurt his back!" She clicked her beak back and forth, keeping up with Mr. Owl. "Do you care to tell me what this is all about?"

"Heathcliff's friend - "

"Yes, I know! We've been through all that. I know him well, but ..."

Mr. Owl nudged his wings into Daisy's, happy with her flying beside him. "I need your help, Daisy. Rasputin has the bear cub and Mr. Mouse. The screams you may have heard were their screams. They both fell into an abandoned well and somehow Rasputin got down inside and grabbed them. We are trying to get there before he eats them all up."

"Well, why didn't you say so?!" Daisy exclaimed. "How can I help?" She spread her wings and flapped hard to keep up with the fast-paced rhythm of Mr. Owl. She was happy to be together again at last, lovingly flying side-by-side as they did every night, playing at high dives and chasing. What fun! But, bringing herself back to the moment, she knew she had to be serious and help in any way she could to save Heathcliff's friend and the bear cub.

She eyed her friend next to her as they swept lower to the ground, in search of some landmark in this fog to make the well easier to find.

"I can take you right to it," Daisy explained. "It's not too far from our tree."

Mr. Owl replied, "I want you to try finding the other owls I called for. They're not too far - in the area of the river that flows behind us. You fly back and lead them to the well. Hurry! We haven't much time!"

Daisy touched his wings lightly in farewell and circled back, flying faster and faster to bring help. She swooped higher in the misty air to keep from colliding into a tree.

"What fun flying is," she mused, scanning the forest carefully. Her ears were alert for anything out of the ordinary, listening for the screeches of the other owls as they hastened to help their friend.

In the JAWS of RASPUTIN

Inside the well, Old Rasputin had the cub as he happily made his way to the old log.

"So you thought to outsmart Old Rasputin," he chuckled, closing his mouth firmly around this chubby creature. "Ahhh! I will have plenty of food this night and a few nights after," he grinned evilly.

The little cub was caught - no doubt about it. He wondered where his new-found friend was. He hoped the little mouse was spared. Sighing wistfully, he tried once to break free, but the wolf had him tight with no chance of escape. If he somehow could go back to sleep, maybe it wouldn't hurt so much when he was being eaten. If only he could see or feel his friend close by ... that would help him through all this.

"Right to the end," the little cub whispered.

Dejectedly, he closed his frightened eyes, his little heart pounding inside Old Rasputin's jaws. *This is it*, he thought, sadly. *Now I will never meet all the friends of the little mouse.*

He was falling asleep from the sheer exhaustion and not being able to breathe very much. Before losing consciousness, he pictured himself

playing in the meadow with the mouse's friends, running among the trees and seeing all the animals accepting him as one of their own. He smiled sadly, knowing it was only a dream. He finally gave in to his exhaustion and slept.

Rasputin made his ascent up the well log as slowly as he had climbed down, finding it extra difficult to hang onto the slippery log with a heavy bear cub in his jaws. *Should eat you now and then be on my way* he thought, *before those pesky owls find me. But then I'd have to eat quickly and this is too good a feast to hurry, then I'd be forced to leave the rest here.*

"No!" he scowled between his teeth. "You are too fine a meal to leave behind. Yes - I will eat all of you."

He took another step up. He could see the first light of dawn as he looked towards the opening above.

"Must hurry," he puffed.

Once daylight came the owls were off his back, but then he'd have to fight the pack ... and he didn't want to work any harder for this feast anymore. It had been a long night and he was growing hungrier by the minute, not to mention weary from all this hassle. He had to hurry out of this hole and run safely back to his lair to feast.

The little cub came awake with a start, his ear suddenly being chewed on. He started to let out a scream, thinking Rasputin was beginning to eat him, but tiny hands held his mouth shut.

"Wake up!" whispered Mr. Mouse, "and be quiet!"

"Must you always bite my ear?" growled the little bear, trying to see where his mouse friend was.

"It's the only way I know to wake you up before Rasputin has you for dinner! You've got to wake up." He tugged again on the sore ear.

46

"All right! Let go of my ear – I'm awake!" whispered the cub in annoyance. "I'm in the wolf's mouth. How do you expect to save us?" He slowly closed his eyes.

"Don't go back to sleep! I can always bite your ear off and then I would have your full attention," urged the little mouse, poking his side. "We can escape, but you have to help me."

The little cub sighed, feeling the old wolf clamping down on him harder as he struggled along the log. "It's too late. I will never get to meet all your friends or get to taste a hive filled with honey, and I will never - OUCH! LET GO!"

Mr. Mouse let go of the ear.

"You can have all those things but you must try to save yourself, cried the little mouse. "You can't give up! I won't let you!" He started patting the sore ear "We can have all those things I told you about, but first we must save ourselves."

Feeling his breathing coming harder and harder, the little cub felt dizzy. He was growing weaker by the second. If he didn't get free of the wolf soon it would be too late, and all his hopeful friends and fun times would be lost forever.

The little mouse was hanging onto his neck, but slowly crawling up to the little cub's worried face.

"We can do it," he said. "Think. Don't fall asleep. Think with me. Together we must at least try."

"Alright," muttered the little cub. "I will think, but only if you promise not to bite my ear anymore." He eyed the mouse sadly, knowing he was growing weaker, his breath coming slower by the second. His ear hurt and he didn't think he could take any more bites on it before it would fall off.

Mr. Mouse looked closely at his new friend, knowing that he was about to be eaten up and too weak to fight the wolf. Gently, he patted the cub's nose, wiping the tears from his eyes. He crept up to the cub's ear again and, slowly, and with the gentle touch of his own ear, whispered, "Ok, you have a deal. I promise not to bite your ear anymore if you will fight off Old Rasputin with me and save us."

Mr. Mouse was frightened and mad at this situation, knowing there was only so much he could do. He tapped his little foot nervously against the cub's nose, making the little bear jump with fear.

"It's ok - just my foot and I trying to figure a way out." He stroked his friend's face. "There must be some way ..."

FRIENDSHIP in the WELL

Wondering what was worse, one ear or being eaten up by this wolf, the little bear cub decided he would much prefer to have two ears and not one. Weakly, he remembered his mom telling him - or rather, teaching him that his ears were the most important part of his body: 'they hear the sounds of the birds, the symphony of the forest, and most importantly, the cry of our enemy - the wolf.'

He imagined he saw his mom and dad, all stern-faced with their big eyes looking down at him.

"Wake up, Sasha, Wake up! You have to save yourself!"

The little cub groaned, as if to answer the distant voice, loving the sound of his parents once more. Opening his eyes, he felt the touch of Mr. Mouse, gentle but firm.

"Did you see them?" the little cub asked, eyes sparkling with joy even though it went unnoticed in the darkness.

"See what?" whispered the little mouse.

"My mom and dad."

"They here?" excitedly asked the mouse, trying not to jump up and down with happiness.

"No, they're dead; I told you that," answered the cub.

"Then why did you say they're here?"

"They *were* here. They called me by my name and told me to fight the mean old wolf."

"And you will!" exclaimed Mr. Mouse, though not really sure that the little cub hadn't imagined all this; but the little mouse was happy with the new spirit of his friend, no matter what he thought he heard, and gleefully accepted what his bear cub friend said.

49

50

"You must always listen to your mom and dad and do what they say."

"Alright," smiled the cub loosely, feeling Rasputin briefly growl after slipping on the log. He lowered his voice again, "My name is Sasha," he proudly stated, all ready to do battle. "And what is your name, Little Pest?"

"My name is Mr. Mouse."

"That's not a name," grinned the cub. "That's what you are."

"That is my name," Mr. Mouse replied, embarrassed. "That's all I have ever been called." Eyeing his friend silently, he shyly asked, "Don't you like my name?"

"I like it very much," answered Sasha, "and if I ever get out of this wolf's mouth, I'll bite you on the ear to show you just how much."

Sasha grunted a slight laugh but knew he was quickly growing weaker, Rasputin's jaws clenching the strength out of him. Mr. Mouse knew this too and was saddened. He had to act fast before he lost his new-found friend.

"Tell me your name once more," he whispered.

Sasha licked his dry mouth, taking in some air. He felt the fangs of Old Rasputin firmly planted around his middle, squeezing the breath from his lungs.

"Sasha," he proudly replied.

"Sasha!" The mouse became so animated he almost slid off the back of his friend, cold and damp from the night's fog. Catching himself and gripping Sasha's neck, he crawled back up, carefully avoiding the sore ear.

51

"Sasha! That is a warrior's name. You are named after the strongest animal that ever lived!" He jumped up and down happily.

"Easy now," muttered Sasha. "What is the meaning of my name - do you know?"

Mr. Mouse joyfully replied, "I most certainly do! It means fighter. The best fighters in the universe. They have been in the jaws of death many, many times! But they fought and escaped! You must fight too and escape!

He jumped down onto the bear's leg, trying to pull him loose from Old  Rasputin's mouth. Sasha had a thought.

"Mr. Mouse," he called, "Mr. Mouse! I have an idea to save us."

Mr. Mouse quickly jumped back up to face Sasha.

"How?" he squealed.

"Be quiet while I tell you. I have a plan and I think it will work! Sasha will save us," he grinned. "I am a warrior." Weakly, he moved his hind end, trying to see if his plan would work.

"I am a warrior," he weakly repeated, trying

to feel strong and powerful. "Now, listen to me carefully because I'm weak and don't want to repeat this. Are you ready?"

"I am ready," shrieked the mouse, his heart pounding with hope. He looked at the top of the well, knowing time was running out and soon Rasputin would be out and making for his feast, "... but Rasputin is almost to the top."

Sasha swallowed, then began, "Now, this is what I want you to do ... "

RASPUTIN'S DINNER

Old Rasputin snickered with glee, listening to the frantic whispers of his soon-to-be meals. It didn't bother him that the mouse was hanging around, as he would make a nice appetizer. *So they think they can outsmart me*, he chuckled to himself. He could almost feel right where the pesty mouse was. *Now, if I can eat him up first, this ball of fur won't put up much fight.*

He hated dealing with problems before his dinner - bad for his digestion and he'd end up spilling out most of it in a fur-ball. Well, this night or dawn, his feast would stay in his belly - he worked hard enough for it.

He grinned to himself, raising his head carefully to the opening outside the well. He knew he had a little time left before the sun came up; cold and a tad exhausted, he dug deeper into the old log and hurried faster. It was wet and getting more slippery by the minute from this nasty fog.

Off in the distance he heard the owls - closer this time. It made him uneasy. He hated dealing with owls. He hated owls - period! Their fierce talons could really do some damage; he remembered all too well. He carried many a scar from being chased and attacked by his winged tormentors.

Old Rasputin took another step up towards the opening, realizing that time was running out. He was very hungry. He was getting nervous. He was getting mad. His stomach growled impatiently.

Now, Old Rasputin was born mean. Anything that ran if front of him, behind him, up in a tree - well, he just had to chase it down and eat it up. He didn't much care what it was. His fearful reputation was important to him and that's all he lived for ... to be feared and to keep his growling belly full. Of course, climbing a tree was not the best thing he could do, but that wasn't saying he didn't try. He enjoyed shaking it from side to side if it wasn't too big, scaring the wits out of the little animals hanging on for dear life. He'd see them and chuckle, raise his large head, and let out a piercing howl before sauntering away, happy he scored again.

It was only a matter of time before the frightened animals came down the tree, their teeth chattering with terror, and then run off into the night

to their warm little beds, safe from that mean old wolf. All the animals in the forest shook with fear upon hearing the howl of Rasputin.

Now, if he was full, he'd chase his prey just for the sport of it and, eating as much as he did, he needed all the exercise he could get. He would growl with glee as the chase went on, seeing their faces full of fear while trying to make it

back to their warm homes, safe for another night. This made Old Rasputin feel more powerful than he already did. And after the chase he'd go back to his den, cocky and more arrogant than ever. He would curl up, majestic head on his paws, and smack his jowls before contentedly falling asleep.

Rasputin was a loner. He was arrogant. He was smug. He was powerful. If he were a tiger he'd be the king of the jungle. But he was a wolf ... and a mean one at that, quite satisfied to be the king of the forest. Yes, Sirree! All the other wolves kept their distance from this one.

The story was that the leader of the pack ran old Rasputin off and warned him never to return. If he dared try coming back and running with them, the whole pack would all fight him. Many times he tried, but ran off limping and yelping back to his own territory where he belonged. He was mean and a bully to all the younger pups in the pack, always causing discontent and too many fights.

Usually, a wolf is a loving, gentle animal, killing only for food to feed themselves and their families. Old Rasputin killed for fun and the thrill of being feared. The pack just wouldn't tolerate this brutal behavior of one of their own and had no choice but to kick him out, before he taught their young all the bad ways of the forest. One Old Rasputin was enough.

Word was, if you see him coming, run in the opposite direction in a pack and not stay and fight the mean one. No-one wanted to fight this one and usually kept their distance. Many a time he was seen by the youngsters in the pack, running at breakneck speed off in the distance, baring his fangs and coming at the pack like an avenging devil - slobbering mouth, eyes wild and deadly, his piercing howl threatening them and daring them to stop him.

One day they would put a stop to Old Rasputin, when they grew stronger and became better fighters - better to match the skills of this wild one ...

The WARRIOR

"Okay! I'm listening!" whispered the little mouse, tugging at the cub's leg. "Tell me what we must do."

"Now first of all, we must distract the wolf from the thought of eating us up."

"Go on," urged Mr. Mouse, "but we have to hurry. Soon he reaches the top and then it's too late."

"Bite his ear," said Sasha.

"Bite his ear! That's ridiculous!" hissed the mouse, quietly as he could manage in his straining voice.

"You got *my* attention with it," Sasha grunted. "It will work on the wolf too."

Mr. Mouse brought his tail around, as he had a habit of doing, when he became nervous. He wrapped it around himself softly and stroked the end while deep in thought.

"What are you doing back there?" the little cub asked weakly.

The mouse replied shakily, "I'm uh … rubbing my tail."

"You just keep on rubbing your tail and soon we'll be eaten up!" Sasha sighed. "I give up."

Mr. Mouse nudged the cub's leg.

"You had me scratch your back because it made you think better. The same with me rubbing my tail."

"Alright, but wake me when we're inside the wolf's tummy. I'm getting sleepy."

"Hey! You wake up! This is no time to sleep!" Mr. Mouse said. "I will bite his ear! Hard! And his screams will make you wide awake!"

Gleefully, the little mouse raced to the top of the cub's head, took a big step back, then leaped onto the wolf's mane, cold and soaked from the fog. Almost losing his step, he grabbed onto the furry neck, taking a deep breath to calm his chattering teeth.

The only time he was this close to a wolf was in his nightmares. His little paws shook uncontrollably as he saw his friend, Sasha, tightly held by those large ferocious teeth, ready to eat him. They were twice as long as the whole length of himself - he shuddered.

He glanced down at his friend, who was staring back at him impatiently. Then, seeing how nervous he was - paws all shaking and eyes wide with fright - he rolled his large brown eyes remorsefully, turning his head back down.

Hopeless to try and escape, Sasha gave in. *Mr. Mouse is just too scared. Soon our worries will be over.*

"I can do it!" shrieked the mouse, not caring if Old Rasputin heard. "Watch me!"

Mr. Mouse took a deep breath of the chilly air and lunged upon Rasputin's head, turning himself upside-down to reach the dingy wet ear. His teeth still chattering, he opened his mouth the widest he had ever done and bit the wolf's ear as hard as he could.

"AAAHHHHOOO!!!!!"

Old Rasputin opened his mouth with painful howls. Sasha was suddenly free of his jaws, fell onto the log, and slid down the wet moss

that covered it. He bounced upon the ground with a thud, rolling into the sleeping possum, who had been asleep and out of sight at its base.

"Oh no, not you again!" the possum grumbled, jumping up and glaring at Sasha. "Have you gone completely mad? Have you no courtesy?" he snorted, wiping his fur with contempt in his fiery eyes.

Sasha grinned, "I told Mr. Mouse to bite Rasputin's ear – and he did it! We were about to be eaten up while you lie here sleeping - while we have been fighting for our lives!"

The possum shivered, looking at the top of the well.

"Why didn't you say so? That mean Old Rasputin, you say?"

"The one and the same," proudly stated Sasha, sticking out his chest and feeling strong and powerful. "The whole forest fears him! Why didn't you know any of this?"

"I do! Oh, but I do! We all f-fear that one!" trembled the possum, eyeing the yelping wolf once more, who was still trying to break free of something hanging on his ear.

The little cub smiled broadly. "My name is Sasha. I am named after a great warrior of the forest. I have been sent to rescue Mr. Mouse."

He enjoyed his moment of triumph, but knew he was going a little overboard. Seeing the doubting look the possum was giving him, he turned away, embarrassed at his lie, but he was happy that he was finally a creature of importance.

"Why aren't you up there?" asked the skeptical possum.

"Well uh ... " Sasha began, "I tangled with the ferocious beast and he knocked me down the log and onto the ground. That's how I rolled into you again. He had a vicious grip on my neck!" He rubbed his neck briefly and continued, stronger than ever: "I let him do it to keep his attention away from Mr. Mouse. Although I was growing weak from his teeth digging into my back, I bit his ear something fierce and kicked him in the leg! And he let go with an awful scream - I lost my balance, reaching out to save my friend, and fell again to the bottom!"

His bright, excited eyes stared at the quiet possum. Smiling, he lowered his voice.

"Being a warrior is not an easy task."

The possum eyed this little creature warily, then yawned, "Aren't you a little young to be such a warrior?"

"Some are born to greatness," Sasha smiled.

Hearing Rasputin scream again, Sasha came to his senses.

"We must hurry and save my friend. Will you help?" Once more, he was a little cub in need of help.

"One so great shouldn't need my help," the possum muttered, having heard just about enough from this highly imaginative little story-teller. A warrior the cub wasn't, but he liked this little one - and even though he had been rudely awaked twice this night by him, he wanted to help in any way he could.

The mouse wasn't much of a meal for Old Rasputin, but he was in bad trouble. Chances were, after the mouse was gulped down, Old Rasputin would slide down the log again and have the little bear and possum for dinner – a feast indeed!

The possum wasn't about to end up in that wolf's belly. Not now and not ever! He glanced into the little cub's eyes and saw a glint of fear. He had to think fast.

"What are your plans, Sasha, oh great warrior?"

The little cub swallowed hard, his heart pounding with fright. He thought he heard owls somewhere off in the distance, but Rasputin was wailing so loud he wasn't sure. He knew it would be just him, the possum, and Mr. Mouse against Old Rasputin.

Looking into the face of the possum, he thought he saw adoration and a bit of hero worship. Happy that he was Sasha again, he smiled broadly.

"First of all, we must distract the wolf from wanting to eat all of us." He thrust out his chest.

"And, just how do we do this?" asked the possum.

"We bite his ear!" grinned the jubilant bear as he started climbing the log up towards mean, Old Rasputin, who was slipping and sliding while trying to shake of Mr. Mouse.

The possum followed close behind, muttering, "I hope this works ... this biting the ear stuff."

The WORRIES of MR. OWL

Rasputin's screams were heard throughout the forest - that was very strange, as usually it was the screams of his victims while they tried to escape from the wolf's jowls.

Heathcliff dug into the owl's sides with all the strength he could muster. He shrieked into Mr. Owl's ear, "That was Rasputin's howl. I know it was!"

"Don't hold so tight! I can't breathe," scolded the owl. "We'll be there in one minute. Daisy will be here soon with the other owls she's leading. I can hear them - maybe it's not too late! Watch for the well Heathcliff! Keep your eyes open!"

"I just can't Mr. Owl! I h-hate this flying!" he replied.

"Open your eyes! If you want to save your friend, you have to help me look for the well!"

The frightened rabbit slowly opened his eyes, seeing the tops of trees up close for the first time.

"Al-alright. T-they're open!"

Heathcliff squinted into the night, searching for the well and his friend – he tried his best to ignore everything else rushing by. How happy he would be when this was over and he and Mr. Mouse would be chasing through the forest again. He would be brave and have a great story to tell his friend when *this* was all over, but maybe this was just a bad dream. He sure wished it was.

Hearing the sounds of the other owls behind them, Heathcliff felt strong, sure everything would be made right, and soon his friend and the little bear would be rescued.

"We'll be there soon, Mr. Mouse. Hang on and know that help is on the way!"

Straining his neck further to see beneath the owl's wing, Heathcliff searched far and wide for the abandoned well, suddenly feeling very lonely for his little friend, and terrified at all the wolfish screams. He sadly wondered if Mr. Mouse was still alive - who the bear cub was – how they met. He never heard Mr. Mouse mention a bear cub he had befriended.

His little head was full of worry and wonder with so many questions not yet answered. He felt the chill and dampness of the night and hoped his friend was warm - wherever he was at this moment.

He shuddered. *Just stay out of the wolf's belly and all will be alright,* he thought.

Another piercing howl filled the night as Mr. Owl swooped lower in a circle, his wings spread wide to slow his descent. If only the fog wasn't so thick, he would be able to see his landmarks. The ground was barely visible and, squinting below, he couldn't even see the tree where Daisy and the other owls were supposed to meet them for the final rescue attempt.

Maybe it really was too late, he thought. He grew saddened ... the little rabbit on his back would be lost without his friend.

Flapping his large wings to shake the terrible mood he was in, he slowly flew from side to side, hoping it would bring some calmness to

Heathcliff. He would keep circling the area, knowing he was not far from the tree and the abandoned well, until he spotted Daisy.

What is keeping her? Nasty, flying in this heavy fog. I can only hope she will fly safely and not be too courageous.

He felt the fast pounding of Heathcliff's heart against his back, scared of flying and so worried about Mr. Mouse. Mr. Owl wished this night was over and everyone was back in their lairs, safe and sound. Sensing that daylight would soon be shining through the night's sky, he thought with sadness that time was running out - soon, nor he or the other owls would be able to help.

A VISIT from SASHA'S ANCESTORS

Old Rasputin was in a lot of
trouble. This pesky little mouse
refused to let go of his grip and,
even shaken roughly, refused to
fall off his neck. The wolf grew
angrier by the minute, baring
his fangs with every attempt to
catch hold of a paw – tail -
ANYTHING he could grasp and
chew up. He was wasting too
much time with this mangy rat
while his hearty feast awaited
him below.

He growled, trying to scare the pest off. Mr. Mouse's response was to
bite hard once again. This time as Rasputin let loose a fearsome cry, Mr.
Mouse lost his balance, skidding down the wolf's back to the damp tail
where he quickly grabbed on to keep from falling. Teeth chattering, he
wondered how he could get back onto Rasputin's head, where he was a
lot safer from those nasty snapping teeth.

Old Rasputin chuckled. Even with the pain he still felt with his ear
bitten so many times, he managed an evil grin.

"Aha! Your life is soon over, you little ugly rodent! I'll get even with
you for what you did to me! Oh yes, I will! And I won't bite just your ear!"

He howled victoriously, knowing soon the mouse and cub would be in
his stomach and he would be running off to his den to get some long-
awaited rest.

"Life is grand!" he snickered as he licked his lips, "Yes, indeed!"

Sasha heard all the commotion overhead and quickened his climb. His little claws dug as deep as they could go into the damp log, his eyes brightly gleaming with vengeance. He would save Mr. Mouse, his new-found friend, and also this short-legged possum, who stuck close to him for protection. He was Sasha! His time had come to be the great warrior! - help all the creatures escape from mean, Old Rasputin! If he had to lose his life saving them, that was his duty.

The little cub shook, knowing it was not from the night's chill. He was so scared - but great warriors weren't supposed to be scared. He hunched his shoulders bravely, climbing on. Mr. Mouse needed him ... but who was going to save himself? Was he born to do this great deed only to die in the end? Sighing, he kept his pace and ambition, knowing what he must do. Only, he felt sad he'd never get to meet Mr. Mouse's friends.

A voice came to him.

"Sasha! Sasha! You are not alone. We are here beside you and will not leave until you are safe with your new friends - away from this mean, old wolf."

The little cub looked around, almost losing his grip on the wet log.

"Easy, my son. Keep climbing to where the old wolf is. You can do this. We will give you the strength. Remember our teachings. Do you remember them?"

"Yes," the little cub gulped, swallowing a tight knot in his throat. The voice was unmistakable – it belonged to his father.

"You are Sasha! A great warrior of the forest like your little friend told you," his dad continued.

"H-how do you know of this?" asked the little bear, watching Rasputin trying to bite at Mr. Mouse, who clung to the wolf's tail.

"We are never far from you. You can't see us anymore, but we are never far from your side."

"How can this be?" Sasha asked. Stopping, he slowly tried to see his mom and dad he loved and missed so much.

"We are here, son," came his mother's voice. *"The great spirit of the heavens brought us back to Earth to watch over you until you are fully grown. Then, and only then, we will return to the sky. Heed what your friend told you. You are a great warrior, Sasha, and right now they need you to save them."*

The little cub roared with his head high, his tears and laughter breaking into the night and stunning Old Rasputin. He pawed the trunk and swayed from side to side with wild abandon, becoming the great warrior indeed.

Rearing up, he pawed at the sky, roaring with vigor and new life.

"Go and do what has to be done. Time is running out. When daylight comes, the owls can't see and you need their help to outsmart Old Rasputin."

72

The little cub looked behind him, feeling slightly embarrassed at his display of being so great a warrior.

"Sorry, Mr. Possum, if I almost made you fall off the log."

"Sorry indeed," snorted the possum, hanging on tightly with his tail.

Sasha's dad spoke, *"Go on, son. You can do this."*

The little cub inhaled deeply, climbing up towards the wolf, who watched him with shock, all fear gone. He caught sight of Mr. Mouse, hanging on for dear life to the wolf's tail. He was weary from trying to stay alive, his little body shaking with fear.

"Mr. Mouse!" Sasha called out.

The little mouse jerked around, blinking his eyes with hope and surprise.

"Sasha!" he squealed. "Boy am I glad to see you!"

"Just hang on! I will save you!"

Sasha happily crept up the log, his face animated with the smell of victory within his reach.

RASPUTIN'S REVENGE

Old Rasputin was furious! No-one chewed on his ear and lived to tell about it! He shook his angry head violently as he tried to shake the miserable rodent off his tail. Growling and twisting his head back, he couldn't quite reach Mr. Mouse. He howled with rage as he jerked from side to side; and in his fit of rage, he lowered his damp, furry rear end to give another sharp shake of his tail.

The wolf angrily stared into the cub's eyes, who stared back with hostility and strength. Both held their eye contact for that single moment, the night quiet and tense. The little cub snorted with anger, pawing into the log.

Mr. Mouse stared down into the well where Rasputin looked, the wolf's body rigid and mean. Bear and wolf challenged each other, still and deadly, ready to fight with all the power left inside them.

"You are about to die," growled the wolf.

"My name is Sasha," slowly replied the cub. "I am going to rescue my little friend, Mr. Mouse, and there is nothing you can do to stop me."

Rasputin roared his head back, his howl loud and humorous.

"You are a very foolish, small morsel of the food chain!"

His mouth slobbering with humor and hunger, he took a step towards the cub. Looking behind this silly creature he saw the possum, close behind, his big eyes scared. He was staying close to the little ball of fur that was the cub.

"So!" he laughed. "You brought your reinforcements! Possums are not known for their courage!" gloated the wolf. "And, from where I'm standing, you are but a wee babe, and one who will be my tastiest meal this night - all easy and tender."

The little cub stopped climbing, but still heard the words of his parents: *"You can do this, Sasha! We are right here by your side."*

He blinked slowly, the wild eyes of the wolf causing him alarm.

"I am Sasha! I am a great warrior. I will fight you and save my friends!"

"No, Sasha!" screamed the little mouse from the flicking tail.

"Run back, little cub!" cried the possum.

"I ... I will not run," stammered the cub, eyes full of fear. "I will stay and help you like you stayed and helped me, Mr. Mouse!"

"You can't fight him," squealed the mouse. "He'll kill you!"

Old Rasputin howled with mockery, "Listen to the runt, you little fur-ball! I will have you for dinner! And after I devour you, I'll eat this mangy thing that bit my ear!"

"I...I am not afraid of you," answered the cub.

"Ha!" shouted the wolf. "You say you do not fear me? Why is it your big, brown eyes, that I will soon have for my dinner, gleam with fear of this big bad wolf?" He laughed wildly, glaring at the two below him.

"I'll tell you what," he slowly added, menace in his voice as he stared down at the shaking cub. "I'll make you a deal!"

"No, Sasha!" yelled the mouse.

"Wh...what kind of a deal?" stammered the little bear.

"Listen to your friend, the mouse," whispered the scared possum. "He's right, you know. You'll die if you fight him."

"I am not afraid," repeated the cub. "What other way is there? What would *you* do?"

The possum looked away before answering, "My legs are short. I could never outrun him. He's right. We are not the bravest of creatures."

"What *would* you do?" repeated Sasha, looking intently into the possum's face.

"Well, I would probably roll into a ball, push myself off the hill, and roll to safety into an old abandoned well."

The bear stared at him.

"You mean that is how you happen to be in this hole?"

"Yes. I have a family out there and, to keep Rasputin from eating us all up, I diverted his attention and rolled and rolled away from my home, finally toppling into this place. Weary, I fell asleep ..." The possum eyed his new friend, clearing his throat, "... until you bounced into me and woke me up!"

"But you saved their lives," gleamed the cub.

RASPUTIN'S DEAL

Down came Rasputin's chilling laugh. It echoed throughout the well like ten evil wolves.

"Hey, you down there! I'm giving you one last chance! I told you I would make you a deal! It's that, or I crawl down and eat you all up!"

The little cub took a deep breath, chest out, ready to do battle.

"I am listening," he said.

The wolf looked down with an evil glint, "Bring me that short-legged creature behind you and I will let you go! I am hungry and have grown tired this night!"

"I … I," stammered the bear cub.

"NOW!" howled the wolf. "Your time is running out!"

Mr. Mouse licked his mouth nervously.

"Run, Sasha! You can climb out while I distract him! And take your possum friend with you!"

"But, how?" asked the cub.

"Silence!" growled Rasputin.

"He can't reach me, Sasha!" Mr. Mouse continued. "Do as I ask! You are a brave warrior! You can do this!"

Already the possum was on the back of the little bear.

"Listen to him," he encouraged. "Your mouse friend can save himself."

"I said SILENCE!" Old Rasputin bellowed. And, for a few moments, the well was still … but the screeches of owls broke the silence.

Rasputin angrily looked at the two below him, "Times up."

He slowly made his descent further down into the dark hole with Mr. Mouse hanging on tightly, trying to climb back to the wolf's ear. It was their only chance! If he could bite Rasputin's ear hard once more, it

should be enough to let the little bear and possum escape. He knew that bears climb better than wolves up deep places.

"Go on, Sasha!" yelled the little mouse. "Now's your only chance! Your last chance! You can do it!"

The little cub looked to Mr. Mouse, the possum, then back at the descending Rasputin, thinking he would at least try. The possum clung onto the cub's back while Mr. Mouse was using his last bit of strength to climb back to the wolf's ear.

Rasputin knew his luck would run out if he didn't rid himself of this rodent that was giving him so much trouble. He was mad that such a little cur like a rat could hold the upper hand.

"No-one can outsmart me!"

Rasputin howled fiercely, rearing back as fast as a deadly cobra to shake the mangy pest free. Mr. Mouse went flying through the air, banging against the stony sides of the well, then hitting the ground. His last thoughts were of his friend, Heathcliff, as he chased him through the brush on their nightly racing games.

"Did you see that?!" shouted Old Rasputin,

80

"Your friend, the rat, is dead!"

He howled with glee, eager to have his dinner and get out of this hole before those musty-smelling owls appeared.

The little cub looked down behind him at the bottom of the well, seeing his friend lying in a heap. He gulped sadly, feeling alone once again and weary. He didn't know what to do, but then the possum spoke.

"Sasha, I'm going back to pick your mouse-friend up. You keep going towards the top. I'll be right back!"

The possum slid off Sasha's back and was gone before the bear could say a word. The little cub looked up at the wolf, now appearing twice the size and ten times as mean as before.

Sasha's dad spoke.

"Go on, Sasha! Remember what we told you. We are right here beside you. Don't be afraid!"

"But ... but he hurt Mr. Mouse. H-He will kill me too and I will never see my new friends again!"

"Sasha! Stop this!" his dad harshly replied. *"You're small but still very strong. Old Rasputin is at a disadvantage. He climbs down and has no sure footing. Bears are fighters! They are warriors as you've been told! Life is not always easy! Sometimes, our strengths are tested, my son."*

The little cub sadly looked around, hoping to see his dad. "I wish I could see you just once more," he muttered. "Since you both left me, I have not had a decent night's sleep and, what strength I do have, has been tested to my limit. I can do no more!"

Rasputin edged forward, barking, "Who are you talking to?!"

"Oh, yes you can," came his mother's voice. *"There are times when the sun does not shine, but soon the dark clouds disappear and the flowers bloom with the first sign of spring. Birds sing and warmth comes to all our dens again."*

Rasputin climbed closer, losing his footing as he tried to grip more firmly into the rotted log. Eyes filled with anger, he stared down at the cub.

"You should have taken my deal," he grinned. "I hear a lot of babbling down there. Keep saying your prayers, runt. The Great Spirit in the heavens can not help you now! This is just between you and I. Your rat-

friend is dead and I can see that cowardly, short-legged creature has already fled."

He howled with glee, smacking his drooling mouth. He was only a few feet away.

The little cub felt a tug on his leg. Not taking his eyes off Rasputin, he felt it again - he knew he had to work fast. His imagination was running wild and he knew Mr. Mouse was probably dead and the possum gone ... they couldn't be tugging on his leg.

"What's the matter, runt? Cat got your tongue?" the wolf bellowed, laughing at his own joke. "I'm coming to get you!"

He advanced closer, enjoying this game. He grinned evilly down at his meal, his tongue licking his jowls - he enjoyed the thought of his tasty dinner but more so watching the fear in the little cub's eyes.

"Now, let me see. Which part of you should I eat first?"

"Psst! Psst!" came a sound from below.

Sasha snorted.

"Psst! Psst!" it repeated.

The little cub felt another tug, and this time felt something slowly crawling up his back. Still not taking his eyes off the wolf, he snorted as if to answer what was happening.

SASHA'S TRANSFORMATION

The Great Spirit *was* here now and was going to help him. He bellowed loudly back at Rasputin - he was the warrior once more. Taken aback, the wolf hesitated at such a change in this little fur-ball.

"Sasha! It's me, Mr. Possum! I have your friend, Mr. Mouse. He is somewhat groggy, but he's alive. He's hanging onto my leg."

"He's alive?" The little cub happily asked, then his father's voice whispered again.

"Son, you must not tarry. Act fast before Old Rasputin can jump down on you. Time is running out. We must leave you. Remember who you are, Sasha – great warrior."

Sasha roared up, scratching out at Rasputin. With all his strength he rocked back and forth, shaking the log beneath them.

"So!" howled the wolf. "You think you can outsmart Old Rasputin! On your knees furball!"

His red eyes glittered with wrath. Debris from the log flew off from the onslaught of the bear. Rasputin teetered from side to side, but his nails were so sharply dug into the battered log that they saved him from falling off. He growled viciously, foam dripping from his angry fangs and onto the cub's face.

"HA! We shall see who the victor is!" gloated the wolf. Slowly, he crouched down on his belly, inching his way towards the cub.

Sasha looked back where he felt the possum. Mr. Possum eyed him in hope.

"I need you to do something," the little cub whispered.

Skeptically, the possum stared back, listening.

"I need you to climb out of the well and take Mr. Mouse to safety."

The possum nodded in relief, happy he wasn't asked to help fight the wolf.

"Climb to the other side of this tree and get out as soon as you can. This old log is tearing up, and soon it will be just me and Old Rasputin. I will be alright. I am strong and I am a warrior!"

Mr. Possum panted, "I will go as fast as I can."

"Take care of Mr. Mouse. Take him safely out of here."

Not hearing a reply, he felt the sliding off his back and knew the possum and Mr. Mouse were heading up out of the well using the underside of the log. He stared at the creeping wolf, almost within reach of him; and, sighing with relief that his friends were safely on their way to freedom, he braced himself for the attack soon to come.

Evil, Old Rasputin, within reach of his dinner once more, stood back up, bracing his body for the attack.

Sasha took a step back, pawing into the log. His own eyes were as cold and deadly as the wolf's as he stared back at his opponent.

Suddenly, he reared himself high to the heavens, letting out a ferocious bear growl, pawing madly towards Rasputin.

Rasputin blinked.

He blinked once more.

Were his eyes going crazy or had this little scrap of meat grown, before his very eyes, into a full-grown bear, mad and with every intent to kill him?

Composing himself, he stared in shock at this grizzly now towering above him. How had he transformed from a mere cub? He knew he had a rough night of it, but had his senses left him out of hunger – was he becoming delusional?

Now, Rasputin was in a fix. Maybe he dallied too long. He loved playing with his prey - a better thing was to torment before the kill, so he thought. Had he waited and tormented too long?

Ears raised, teeth bared, he let out his last howl before the death plunge. Leaping into the bear, paws lashing out, he bit onto the throat - he held tightly, tearing into flesh.

Sasha let out a piercing scream, flinging his paw heavily down on top of the wolf's head, knocking them both to the ground. The temporary dizziness from the fall was quickly replaced with battle-rage. Rasputin circled, bearing his teeth to tear into the bear again.

The little cub stood upright and pawed at him again as he challenged the wolf to make his next attack, shaking his head from side to side as blood flowed down the side of his chest.

Rasputin lunged again, biting into the cub's hind leg as Sasha brought his front paws down with the speed of surprise, pummeling Rasputin to the ground.

The wolf gasped with alarm at the bear's swiftness. He jumped back up, stunned, but angry enough to kill this bear once and for all.

Bear and wolf growled, each circling the other, ready for the next strike.

"You're about to die – just like your rat-friend!" snarled Rasputin.

Sasha sent a piercing scream throughout the well. "I am Sasha! I will not die! I will be the victor and, if I have to, I will kill you so you can't hurt the creatures of the forest ever again!"

He was bleeding …but he would not give up.

SASHA'S STRENGTH

"Ha! You don't stand a chance!" the wolf snickered. "No-one fights Rasputin and lives to tell about it!" Drool dripped from his mouth.

Sasha roared, "I am no longer afraid of you! You have hurt my friend! Now you will get what you deserve!"

He lunged at the wolf, jaw wide as he flung his massive paw and knocked Rasputin to the ground yet again. The screech of owls filled the air over the blaring sound of their cries. They flew around the well and down into the hole, circling Rasputin's

90

head in a sound of wings and chaos – all attacking Rasputin.

Rasputin kept his head down, knowing he could never fight off all these frantic pests. How he hated owls! Seeing the log, he raced to it, howling all the way to the top. Once out, he looked back down.

"Another time, you mangy piece of fur! This isn't over!"

Seeing the owls fly up towards him he let out a vicious howl and raced off into the night, angry and still very hungry, back to his den. Daisy chased him for a good distance, nipping him in the flanks. Enjoying his yelps, she gave him one last bite before flying happily back to join her friends.

Heathcliff jumped off Mr. Owl's back, running to Sasha. "You ... you must be my friend's friend!" he squealed. "Tell me, where is Mr. Mouse? Is he all right?"

The little cub smiled, "Yes, Mr. Mouse is safe. Mr. Possum carried him to the top and out to safety, away from mean, Old Rasputin."

"Is he hurt? Did Rasputin hurt him?"

"Now, now," Mr. Owl chimed in. "Your friend is alright. In just a minute we'll all join him. Right now, there are other matters to contend with."

Hearing the noise of all the other owls, he flapped his wings to get their attention.

"Quiet! We have all had a very busy night of it. From what I can gather, we owe this wee cub our thanks for fighting Old Rasputin and saving his friends. He was very brave and deserves our praise."

Mr. Owl eyed Sasha with great pride at his bravery. "How did you do it?" he asked, perplexed even for an owl.

Heathcliff chimed in, "What is your name? Thank you for saving Mr. Mouse's life. He is my -"

Mr. Owl interrupted, "Now Heathcliff, I think this little cub deserves his say; and then, let's be on our way and get out of this well. Soon it'll be daylight and we have to seek cover."

The little cub stepped forward, proud and happy.

"My name is Sasha!"

"How did you fight off Old Rasputin," they all asked in wonder. "You are but a cub. He's the meanest wolf in the forest. Everyone fears him!"

93

The little cub smiled triumphantly, "I hit him here!" he laughed. "Then I hit him here!" He stood tall, batting his paws back and forth, showing how he fought the mean, old wolf.

"All alone? You are a hero!" the owls repeated, eyes even wider than normal with awe and worship.

"I had some help," Sasha replied, a bit embarrassed at his display. "Mr. Mouse is the real hero. He kept biting the wolf's ear and helped me fight Rasputin. I couldn't have done it without him. He got hurt," he glanced at Heathcliff, "- but he'll be alright. You have a great friend. Mr. Mouse saved my life."

The owls moved closer, along with Heathcliff, scanning his neck to see where the blood was flowing down the little cub's throat and neck – they saw his wounds when they flew down into the well – but now they saw no blood and, puzzled at the transformation from grizzly back into cub, they frowned.

"When we flew in here there was a grizzly. Then we chased Rasputin out and now - we see a cub. What happened?"

"Yes. Rasputin tore at my throat. I bled and thought he had won the battle and would kill me. But, somehow I became very strong and tore back into him. We fought long and hard until you came to my rescue. I'm so glad you did," he smiled, "for I was growing weary from losing so much blood. Now, let's go see Mr. Possum and Mr. Mouse. I too have grown very fond him."

"But first, tell us how you were a grizzly one minute and the next a wee cub!"

They all spoke in unison, excitement on their faces.

"My name, Sasha, means 'great warrior'. I know this because Mr. Mouse told me. My Earth parents visited me and they told me the Great Spirit would give me strength and protect me."

"But," said Mr. Owl, frowning, "where are they - your Earth parents?"

Sasha replied, "They are dead. Shot by men carrying large guns. I was left to die. I wandered around lost, and then Mr. Mouse ran into me, knocking us both in here. We tumbled and tumbled, rolled and rolled," he exclaimed, his eyes bright with pride once more, " ... and then - what seemed like forever – we came tumbling down into this well, bouncing against the sides of the ... "

Seeing all their faces, he smiled, not noticing that they were becoming weary.

"Well, anyway, we bounced into Mr. Possum. You see? That's how we all met each other."

The owls looked at each other, wondering if Sasha would ever be quiet. A chatterbox he was, and here it was almost morning and they were exhausted, needing to hide in their trees before the sun rose.

"And then ..." the cub exclaimed, all eager to tell the rest of his adventure.

Mr. Owl broke in, "Ahem, dear Sasha, save some of your great tale for tomorrow when we are all rested. Get on my back again, Heathcliff. We must go and find your friend now."

"Yes," Sasha agreed, blushing.

Heathcliff jumped onto Mr. Owl's back, not as afraid this time.

"I am ready!"

All the owls flew out of the dark hole, Mr. Owl and Daisy leading the way.

The little cub followed, climbing back up the tattered log and happily walking free of the well.

The BIG CELEBRATION

Mr. Possum was waiting in the thicket, surrounded by all the forest animals who came out to find out what had happened, and what all the

commotion was about. Mr. Mouse, fully recovered from his fall, squealed when he saw his friend again. Heathcliff jumped off the owl, hopping over to his friend.

"Mr. Mouse! I am so happy to see you! How I have missed you!"

They hugged each other as Sasha looked on sadly, thinking his time here was over and that he had to move on. His big eyes watched the happy reunions as he swayed from side to side, seeing all the happiness of these creatures of the forest.

Mr. Mouse looked around, eyeing the little cub. His face lit up with relief and joy, racing over to jump onto Sasha's back. He announced to

the others. "This is my other friend and I want him to be yours, too. He fought bravely and saved my life. He is a great warrior!" He tugged at the cub's ear and chuckled, "Sasha is the bravest I have seen. He fought old Rasputin! Rasputin planned on killing this little cub, but Sasha

became big - strong and powerful like the grizzlies we see from time to time."

Cheers went up all around: the squirrels tapped their tails, ducks quacked in joy, deer pranced their hooves – all celebrated the victory over Old Rasputin. The owls flapped their wings in honor and farewell as they began to fly to their homes. The sun was starting to break through the fog so they flew away to the safety of the trees, pairing off with their mates, with Daisy and Mr. Owl planning some long overdue sleep.

"Welcome to our family!" all the animals cheered.

"After we all rest some in our lairs," Heathcliff began, "we'll introduce you to our other friends of the forest. Meanwhile, you can come to my lair with Mr. Mouse," he happily invited.

The little cub was happy. He was safe, had some new friends, and knew his Earth parents were watching over him. He looked to the heavens, searching into the fog until finally he saw them.

His dad's voice entered his ears.

"You're safe, son. The Great Spirit has kept you from harm and you will grow into a fine, powerful bear. I am proud of you. Now you have your friends of the forest to bring you happiness."

Slowly, they disappeared. Sasha raised his paw as if trying to reach them, but they smiled down at him until they were gone. He snorted a farewell, feeling sad for a moment. Then, looking at his new friends, who were watching him with mystery and hero-worship, he smiled and swayed from side to side.

Mr. Mouse scratched the bear's back as they walked back into the forest all together, excited and eager to get some sleep so they would be refreshed for tomorrow's games.

The little cub grinned. He was home.

THE END

Author's Words

    I am a new author. Frustrated at trying to make a living as a voice-over actress, I decided to pursue a hidden dream I have had since a child – To Write! A couple of years ago, I tapped into those desires and my heart and mind reached forth together to find the solace and satisfaction to my being that I crave and need.

    Up in the mountains, surrounded by trees and peaks hovering high above me, I hike, I snowshoe, and I track the mountain lion – breathing the same air as they, communicating and appreciating their greatness. Animals have fed me with spiritual food all of my life that has filled me with adventure and purity of mind, body, and spirit.

    I live in the Susannah Pass Mountains, in West Hills, CA. with my two feline friends – "Heathcliff" and "Rasputin." My goals are to continue writing and to keep involved with saving the wolf and other wildlife from the human threats of greedy corporations and politicians...to help preserve the land they need - to help in making sure the balance is kept between man and beast.

Jennifer Miller is the author of:
Novel 1 – "Sweet Revenge"
Novel 2 – "Marooned"
Novel 3 – "Autumn Run" (unfinished)
Novels 4,5,& 6 – "Run, Rasputin Run!" Books I, II, & III
                (Books 2 & 3 of the Trilogy to bc released next year)

ISBN 1-41206430-9